Gary Grasshopper
DISCO DANCES

Written by Connie Amarel
Illustrated by Swapan Debnath

This book is dedicated in loving memory of my beloved best friend Kathy; may there be many more adventures awaiting us when we reunite in the future. It is also dedicated with much love and appreciation to my wonderful family for all their love and support and to my friend Aimme for her excellent suggestion. Lastly, it is dedicated with deepest gratitude and many thanks to my incredibly talented illustrator Swapan.

Gary Grasshopper yawned, stretched and hopped out of bed. He was grinning from ear to ear because his best friend, Freddie Firefly, was coming to visit today.

Gary opened the curtains and saw that it was a perfect day for his friend to come. The last time he saw Freddie was during Spring Break.

Gary couldn't wait to tell Freddie about the dance on Friday night and about his friends, Florinda Flea and Amelia Ant, who would be there. He knew that Freddie would like them a lot.

He was anxious for Freddie to meet his new friends, Madison Mole and Gopher Glenn. Freddie would be surprised to hear that Gary met them when he fell down a mole hole while playing kickball at the park.

Gary also planned to introduce Freddie to his dance instructor, Olivia Owl, the best dance instructor around. Gary was an excellent hopper, but when it came to dancing, he had two left feet.

Olivia was teaching Gary many dances, but he liked doing the Disco best. He was sure that if he could learn to Disco really well, he would be able to impress everyone attending the dance.

Gary danced down the sidewalk and headed toward the park. He was meeting Freddie there. Buster Beetle, Inchy Inchworm, Tommy Termite, Betty Butterfly and Chris Caterpillar would be there, too.

They were so excited to see Freddie again. After meeting at the park, they would go to Gary's house for pizza and root beer floats. Gary wanted to show them some of the dance moves he had learned.

Gary's friends were waiting when he arrived at the park. They hugged and began their watch for Freddie. Soon Betty Butterfly announced that she could see Freddie in the distance.

Everyone ran to greet Freddie and he ran toward them, too. He hugged Gary first and then hugged the rest of his friends. They talked and laughed as they headed to Gary's house.

They sat on the living room floor eating pizza and drinking root beer floats. Gary asked Freddie how he was doing at school.

Freddie told him that Carl Cockroach had become one of the nicest students there. Carl made sure that no one was bullied at school. He and Freddie were now good friends.

They talked about the dance on Friday. Gary told them he was taking dance lessons with Olivia Owl. They all were anxious to see Gary's dance moves.

Gary was more than happy to show them. He had them move back to give him plenty of room. Inchy put on Disco music and Gary began to dance.

He flung his arm and kicked his leg, which accidentally hit Tommy. Gary told Tommy he was sorry for kicking him but Tommy said it didn't hurt.

Gary did a spin move and hit Buster with his foot. Gary said he was sorry to Buster and hoped he wasn't hurt. Buster said he didn't even feel it.

Gary started dancing again but stepped on Inchy's toe. He told Inchy he was sorry and asked if his toe was all right. Inchy said it was and that Gary didn't need to keep saying he was sorry.

Gary explained that he needed to say he was sorry. He felt really bad about stepping on Inchy's toe, kicking Buster and hitting Tommy, even if it was an accident.

Gary said that he cared about them a lot and that saying he was sorry made him feel better, too. Everyone there agreed that saying you're sorry does make you feel better.

They watched eagerly as Gary finished the dance and then stood up and clapped for their friend. Gary took a bow and thanked them all.

They decided to meet at the park on Friday so that they could all go to the dance together. Gary and Freddie hugged their friends and said goodbye.

Gary had a dance lesson in the morning. He told Freddie he was so excited to have him meet Olivia Owl. Freddie was hoping that she could show him a few dance moves, too.

Freddie and Gary talked for most of the night. The next morning they had a quick breakfast and then went to see Olivia Owl. She was waiting at the dance studio and Gary introduced her to Freddie.

Freddie said he was so happy to meet her and that she had taught Gary wonderful dance moves. He watched Gary and Olivia dancing and thought she glided across the floor like a beautiful princess.

Gary told Olivia about accidentally stepping on Inchy's toes, kicking Tommy and hitting Buster when he showed them his Disco moves. Olivia showed him how to do the Disco moves in a more gentle way.

She asked Freddie what dance he would like to learn. He said he would like to learn the Jitterbug. Gary and Freddie spent the afternoon dancing with their wonderful instructor.

Before they left, Gary told Olivia about the dance on Friday night and invited her to come. She said she would definitely try to be there so she could watch them dance.

Friday night came quickly. Gary and Freddie dressed up for the dance. They hurried to the park where their friends were waiting for them. They all headed to the dance together.

The dance had already started when they got there. They saw Madison Mole and Gopher Glenn on the dance floor doing the Twist.

When the song was over, Gary introduced Madison and Glenn to Freddie. He told Freddie about falling down the mole hole.

Freddie told them he was so happy to meet them and how wonderful it was that they helped Gary. He told them they looked great doing the Twist.

They both said thanks and then Glenn smiled. He said that every time he does the Twist, his stomach says thank you very much. Everyone thought that was funny.

Gary saw Florinda Flea and Amelia Ant standing by the dessert table. He quickly hopped over and said he wanted them to meet his best friend.

He introduced them to Freddie and they talked and laughed. A Jitterbug started to play and Freddie asked Florinda to dance. She said yes.

Gary told Amelia he couldn't do the Jitterbug very well, but he would try if she wanted to dance. She said she would love to, so they headed onto the dance floor.

Everyone was having a wonderful time and before they knew it, the DJ announced that he was going to play the last song of the evening.

Gary's heart sunk because he realized he didn't get to do his Disco dance. He broke into a big smile as soon as he heard the music. It was a Disco song.

Gary spun around and started to Disco the way Olivia Owl had taught him. He did gentle moves so that he wouldn't kick anyone or step on any toes.

Everyone at the dance stopped to watch Gary. He looked over and saw Olivia Owl watching him, too. She was smiling because she was so proud of him.

When the song ended, they all cheered and clapped for Gary. He took a bow and said thank you. He was grinning from ear to ear.

The loudest cheering and clapping came from Gary's friends, especially Freddie Firefly. Freddie was so proud of Gary and felt so lucky to be his friend.

On the way to Gary's house the light in Freddie's tail was shining brightly. He smiled as he watched Gary Disco dance down the sidewalk. He knew they'd be best friends forever.